Dothraki

A Conversational Language Course
Based on the Hit Original HBO® Series
Game of Thrones

by David J. Peterson

LIVING LANGUAGE ®

Published in the United States by Living Language, an imprint of Random House LLC, a Penguin Random House Company.

Publisher: Amanda D'Acierno
Product Managers: Dan Zitt and Sue Daulton
Editors: Suzanne McQuade and Erin Quirk
Production Editor: Ciara Robinson
Production Manager: Tom Marshall
Managing Editor: Alison Skrabek
Production Design: Ann McBride
Interior Design: Sophie Chin and Tina Malaney
Audio Producer: Ok Hee Kolwitz
Designer: Ryan Sacks
Special thanks as well to HBO team members Joshua Goodstadt, Janis Fein, Jeff Peters, Cara Grabowski, and Stacey Abiraj.

www.livinglanguage.com
First Edition
ISBN: 978-0-8041-6086-5
This book is available at special discounts for bulk purchases for sales promotions or premiums. Special editions, including personalized covers, excerpts of existing books, and corporate imprints, can be created in large quantities for special needs. For more information, write to Special Markets/Premium Sales, 1745 Broadway, MD 3-1, New York, New York 10019 or e-mail specialmarkets@randomhouse.com.
PRINTED IN THE UNITED STATES OF AMERICA
10 9 8 7 6 5 4 3 2 1

Course Outline

About Dothraki

Athchomar chomakea!
Welcome!

Before you get started learning Dothraki, you may want to know a bit of the history of the language. In the summer of 2009, the creators of HBO's *Game of Thrones*, Dan Weiss and David Benioff, approached the Language Creation Society about creating the Dothraki language for the show's pilot. What followed was an intense, two-round application process which saw some of the best language creators from around the world competing to be the official language creator for the show. After two rounds of judging, David Peterson's 300-page Dothraki proposal was accepted, and he got straight to work translating dialogue for the pilot.

Now that you know the real history of the language, fictionally the Dothraki language is spoken by the Dothraki: a population of loosely confederated bands of horse-riding warriors who make their home on the steppes of Essos. Dothraki is a lightly inflectional language related to the Lhazareen language, and can be used by a number of residents of the Free Cities, many of whom live in fear of Dothraki raiding parties. The Dothraki have no writing system and no use for books. In this book we'll make use of a Romanization system to write the language, but bear in mind that it's a spoken language first and foremost. To be appreciated properly it needs to be spoken aloud. Forcefully.

How To Use This Course

This course is designed to be used linearly, beginning with Pronunciation and ending with the Dialogue and Exercises. Repeat sections as often as you need to until you have a good grasp of the content: repetition is key to learning any language.

The audio that comes with this course is meant to be used with the book to reinforce your understanding of the complexities of Dothraki pronunciation. The Basic Expressions, Grammar, and Dialogue audio sections also include English translations of each Dothraki word or phrase so that you can use this part of the audio on the go.

Lesson 1

Pronunciation

1: Pronunciation

Before you start speaking Dothraki, you'll need to know how to pronounce it. This course uses the Romanized version of Dothraki, and while most letters are pronounced as they are in English, there are some key differences. See the charts below for examples of Dothraki pronunciation. Please note that many Dothraki words have multiple pronunciation variants, often depending on whether the speaker is native or non-native. **Khaleesi**, for example, has three separate pronunciations: **khal-eh-si**, **khal-ee-si**, and **kal-ee-si**. You will also hear both **khal** and **kal** used for the word **khal**.

DOTHRAKI	ENGLISH EXAMPLE	DOTHRAKI EXAMPLES
a	between hat and hot; hot (after q)	astat *to say* qacha *firefly*
ch	mischief	chare *ear* sachat *to divide* M'ach! *Hi!*

DOTHRAKI	ENGLISH EXAMPLE	DOTHRAKI EXAMPLES
d	dog (dental)	**dothralat** *to ride* **adakhat** *to eat*
e	grey; bed (after q)	**eveth** *water* **qevir** *forest*
f	feather	**fonak** *hunter* **hlofa** *wrist, ankle* **darif** *saddle*
g	good	**Gwe!** *Here!/Let's go!/Go!* **khogar** *clothes*
h	hand	**haj** *strong* **tihat** *to look, to see* **rhoa** *animal* **fih** *smoke*

DOTHRAKI	ENGLISH EXAMPLE	DOTHRAKI EXAMPLES
i	machine; grey (after q)	iz *poison* fati *insult* qile *island*
j	jungle	jahak *braid* lajak *warrior* haj *strong*
k	sky	ko *bodyguard* akat *two* fonak *hunter*
kh	Bach	khefat *to sneeze* zhikhat *to be sick* rikh *rotten*

DOTHRAKI	ENGLISH EXAMPLE	DOTHRAKI EXAMPLES
l	leg (dental)	**lajak** *warrior* **malilat** *to be finished* **krol** *flea*
m	man, jam	**m'athchomaroon** *hello* **mem** *sound*
n	no, men (dental)	**ninthqoyi** *blood sausage* **majin** *and then, then*
o	open; not (after q)	**okeo** *friend* **qora** *hand, arm*
q	sky, but produced deep in the back of the throat	**qora** *hand, arm* **oqooqo** *heartbeat* **fasqoyi** *destiny*

DOTHRAKI	ENGLISH EXAMPLE	DOTHRAKI EXAMPLES
r	rolled, as in Spanish, when at the beginning of the word and followed by a vowel, at the end of the word, or when doubled; everywhere else, tapped	**rai** *hooray* **rhaesh** *land, country* **mori** *they* **mhar** *sore* **jerriya** *discussion* **mithri** *rest*
s	see	**sajo** *one's own horse* **ase** *word, command* **vaes** *city*
sh	she	**shierak** *star* **kisha** *we* **hosh** *giddyup*

DOTHRAKI	ENGLISH EXAMPLE	DOTHRAKI EXAMPLES
t	stop (dental)	tih *eye* ataki *first* astat *to say*
th	thin	thir *alive* athrokar *fear* eveth *water*
v	very, have	vov *weapon* havzi *cat*
w	water, anyway	awazak *screamer* zoqwat *to kiss*
y	yes, boy	yer *you (sg.)* qoy qoyi *blood of my blood*

DOTHRAKI	ENGLISH EXAMPLE	DOTHRAKI EXAMPLES
z	zoo	ziso *wound* kazga *black* laz *could, can*
zh	measure	zhavorsa/ zhavvorsa *dragon* afazhi *warm* rizh *son*

Double Consonants and Vowels

Whenever you see a consonant or vowel doubled in Dothraki, each segment is pronounced fully. For consonants, think about how you say the letter *s* in the words *misunderstood* versus *misspent*.

dd	addrivat *to kill*
ff	affin *when*
gg	rhaggat *cart*

hh	najahheya *victory*
jj	ajjalan *tonight*
kk	akka *also, as well*
ll	jelli *cheese*
mm	gomma *mouth*
nn	hanna *rose*
qq	jaqqa *executioner*
rr	tolorro *bone*
ss	disse *only, just*
tt	esittesak *braggart*
vv	inavva *sister*
ww	ewweya *olive pit*
yy	ayyathat *to lift*

zz	ezzolat
	to teach

Remember that this distinction is important, as the doubling of a consonant can change the meaning of a word.

jelli
cheese

jeli
lemon

When consonants such as **ch, kh, sh, th**, and **zh** are doubled, they become **cch, kkh, ssh, tth**, and **zzh** respectively.

cch	vosecchi
	of course not
kkh	lakkhat
	to chew
ssh	asshekh
	today
tth	atthirar
	life
zzh	Havazzhifi Kazga
	Black Salt Sea

In vowel clusters, each vowel sound is pronounced consecutively, whether the vowels are the same or different. This means that a word like **krazaaj** technically has three syllables (kra–za–aj), all given full voice. Any vowel can appear next to any other vowel. Some (but not all) examples are shown below.

aa	krazaaj *mountain*
ae	vaes *city*
ee	avees *father (accusative)*
ei	dei *shallow*
ia	chelsian *locust*
io	chiori *woman*
oa	choakat *to be bitter*
oo	m'athchomaroon *hello*

As an important spelling note, in reading George R. R. Martin's series *A Song of Ice and Fire*, you may occasionally come across a Dothraki word that utilizes the spelling **jh**, such as **Jhogo**, one of Khal Drogo's bloodriders. In developing a consistent Romanization system for the HBO series, the spelling **jh** was respelled **zh**. Thus, what is spelled **Jhogo** in the books will be spelled **Zhogo** here, and vice versa.

Stress

Stress is the emphasis placed on syllables in spoken language. In English, just think about how you say the word *EMphasis*: the stress falls on the first syllable. Generally, stress in Dothraki follows these rules:

When a word ends in a vowel, the stress falls on the first syllable: ataki, havzi

When a word ends in a consonant, the stress falls on the final syllable: lajak, m'athchomaroon

When the penultimate syllable is a heavy syllable (a syllable that consists of a consonant-vowel-consonant combination before another consonant) and the word ends in a vowel, the penultimate syllable will be stressed: zhavorsa, vosecchi

There are a few other exceptions to the above rules, but these rules will cover most of the new words you'll come across in Dothraki. Listen carefully to the audio that comes with this course to hear the proper stress on words.

LESSON 2

BASIC EXPRESSIONS

2: Basic Expressions

Greetings and Parting Expressions

To begin with, you should know how to greet a person in Dothraki. We'll learn more about how some of these individual expressions work grammatically later in this course; for now, just memorize these as set expressions.

M'athchomaroon!
Hello! (lit.: *With respect!*)

M'ath!/M'ach!
Hi! (short for **M'athchomaroon!**)

Athchomar chomakaan!
Hello! (to a non-Dothraki, singular) (lit.: *Respect to one that is respectful!*)

Athchomar chomakea!
Hello! (to non-Dothraki, plural) (lit.: *Respect to those that are respectful!*)

Aena shekhikhi!
Good morning! (lit.: *Morning of light!*)

To ask how someone is doing in Dothraki, say:

Hash yer dothrae chek?
How are you? (lit.: *Do you ride well?*)

To answer this question, you can say:

Anha dothrak chek.
I'm fine. (lit.: *I ride well.*)

To say *goodbye* in Dothraki, use one of the following expressions:

Fonas chek!
Goodbye! (lit.: *Hunt well!*)

Hajas!
Goodbye! (lit.: *Be strong!*)

Dothras chek.
Be cool. (lit.: *Ride well.*)

⊕ Culture Note
GREETINGS

The Dothraki are notoriously mistrusting of outsiders, and so they have different greetings for fellow Dothraki and for greeting foreigners, or **ifaki**. (The word **ifaki** is considered derogatory in Dothraki.) When greeting fellow riders in their own **khalasar**,

Dothraki will use the expression **m'athchomaroon** meaning *respect*. For **ifaki**, they will use the expression **Athchomar chomakaan/chomakea!** which literally means *Respect to one that is respectful!* This greeting serves as a warning to outsiders: respect us, and you will be treated with respect. Otherwise, watch out.

Fighting Expressions

There are also many expressions used in Dothraki for fighting. To encourage fellow warriors, Dothraki use the following expressions:

Shieraki gori ha yeraan!
The stars are charging for you!

Fichas jahakes moon!
Get him! (lit.: *Take his braid!*)

You can also use the following phrases to express disagreement:

Yer ojila!
You're wrong!

Anha efichisak haz yeroon!
I disagree!

When Dothraki are feeling merciful toward their enemies, they might say:

Anha vazhak yeraan thirat.
I will let you live.

⊕ Culture Note
BATTLE

The Dothraki don't believe in money, but instead take what they want through war and plunder, going into battle and enslaving the defeated survivors. The Dothraki people use a variety of weapons in battle, the most common being the **arakh**, a curved sword. Other weapons used by the Dothraki include whips (**orvik**), bow (**kohol**) and arrow (**laqam**), daggers (**mihesof**), and bolas (**gehqoyi**). The Dothraki do not wear armor as it impedes their speed and motion in battle. Dothraki attacks are most often mounted from horseback; they almost never attack on foot. They value strength above all else. All Dothraki warriors (**lajaki**) wear their hair in a braid (**jahak**). It is only cut when they are defeated, to signify their shame. Neither blood nor weapons may be drawn inside the walls of **Vaes Dothrak**, the Dothraki city.

Being a tribe of warriors, the Dothraki have many different reasons for killing. Thus, there are multiple verbs in Dothraki that mean *to kill*: **addrivat, drozhat,** and **ogat** are some of the most common. **Addrivat** literally means *to make something dead* and is used when the killer is a sentient being. **Drozhat** is used most often when the killer is an animal or an inanimate object, like a fallen rock.

Drozhat is also used when a person kills another person in a fit of insanity, meaning he or she was acting more like an animal than a human. Finally, **ogat** means *to slaughter* and is used mostly for the act of killing animals.

Friendly Expressions

Of course, you can also use these gentler expressions in Dothraki when talking with someone friendly.

Yer zheanae.
You're beautiful.

Yer allayafi anna.
I like you. (lit.: *You please me.*)

Anha zhilak yera.
I love you.

Yer shekh ma shieraki anni.
You are my loved one. (to a male) (lit.: *You are my sun and stars.*)

Yer jalan atthirari anni.
You are my loved one. (to a female) (lit.: *You are the moon of my life.*)

Asshekhqoyi vezhvena!
Happy birthday! (lit.: *[Have] a great blood-day.*)

Anha zalak asshekhqoyi vezhvena yeraan!
I wish you a happy birthday! (lit.: *I wish you a great blood-day!*)

There is also the word **shekhikhi,** which is the diminutive of **shekhikh** (*light*). Literally **shekhikhi** means *little light,* and is used by parents as a term of endearment for their children.

⊕ Culture Note
SUN AND MOON

Take another look at the following expressions:

Yer shekh ma shieraki anni.
You are my loved one. (to a male) (lit.: *You are my sun and stars.*)

Yer jalan atthirari anni.
You are my loved one. (to a female) (lit.: *You are the moon of my life.*)

These expressions come from Dothraki mythology, in which the sun is the husband of the moon.

Other Basic Expressions
Let's look at some additional useful basic expressions.

sek
yes

Sekosshi!
Definitely!

vos
no

Vosecchi!
No way!

San athchomari yeraan!
Much respect! (lit.: *A lot of honor to you!*)

Athdavrazar!
Excellent! (lit.: *Usefulness!*)

Hajas!
Cheers! (lit.: *Be strong. Also used in parting.*)

Hazi davrae.
That's good.

Hazi vo mra zhor.
I don't care. (lit.: *That's not in my heart.*)

M'athchomaroon, zhey Drogo!
Hello, Drogo! (lit.: *With respect, O Drogo!*)

In Dothraki, when you address someone directly, you place zhey directly before their name or title. It's also used to respectfully introduce a third party into a conversation by name. An example is given below.

Anha tih avees yeri, zhey Zhaqo, asshekh.
I saw your father Zhaqo today.

⊕ Culture Note
EXPRESSING THANKS

There is no Dothraki word for *thank you*. As you saw above, there are ways of expressing respect in a way that we might think of as thanks, but it is more a term reflecting wishes of honor to the listener.

San athchomari yeraan!
Much respect! (lit.: *A lot of honor to you!*)

In general, the Dothraki have a strong sense of honor and respect. While they don't trade, per se, they will accept tribute such as gold, and will honor that gift in return. However, they will do so at their own leisure.

LESSON 3
GRAMMAR

3: Grammar

Personal Pronouns

Personal pronouns are words that replace nouns: *I, you, he, she, it*, etc.

Before we get too far in discussing pronouns, you need to know that the Dothraki language marks case. This means that the nouns and adjectives change depending on their use in the sentence—subject, direct object, indirect object, etc. You'll learn the other cases later, but for now, we'll just look at the nominative case of the personal pronouns, which you will use when the pronoun is a subject: *I go, you are*.

	SINGULAR	PLURAL
First Person	anha *I*	kisha *we*
Second Person*	yer *you* (familiar singular)	yeri *you* (familiar plural)
	shafka *you* (formal plural and singular)	
Third Person	me *he/she/it*	mori *they*

*Note that the second-person pronoun for *you* changes depending on number and formality. When speaking to one person, you'll use yer; when speaking to multiple people, you'll use yeri, similar to how you might say *you all* or *you guys* in English. In more formal situations, you will use shafka for both singular and plural *you*.

Verbs: –lat Verbs in the Present Tense

You just learned the pronouns, but if you want to use them in complete sentences, you'll need to know some verbs to go with them! Verbs in Dothraki are conjugated based on person and number, meaning their endings will change depending on the number and person of the subject. There are many types of verbs in Dothraki. To begin with, we'll look at regular –lat verbs. To conjugate a –lat verb in Dothraki, form the stem of the verb by dropping the infinitive suffix (–lat), and then add these endings for the present tense:

	SINGULAR	PLURAL
First person	–k	–ki
Second person	–e	–e
Third person	–e	–e

Let's look at one of the most useful Dothraki –lat verbs: **dothralat** (*to ride*). In the present tense, **dothralat** (stem: **dothra–**) will conjugate as follows:

	SINGULAR	PLURAL
First person	dothrak	dothraki
Second person	dothrae	dothrae
Third person	dothrae	dothrae

You may have seen this verb used before:

Khalakka dothrae mr'anha!
A prince rides inside me!

Now let's look at how this works with the pronouns you just learned.

Anha dothrak.
I ride.

Yer dothrae.
You (sg.) ride.

Me dothrae.
He rides.

Kisha dothraki.
We ride.

Yeri dothrae.
You (pl.) ride.

Mori dothrae.
They ride.

Shafka dothrae.
You (sg./pl. fml.) ride.

Note that **shafka** always takes the third person plural agreement.

Here are some other verbs that conjugate similarly to **dothralat**.

assilat (stem: **assi–**)	*to signal*
astilat (stem: **asti–**)	*to joke*
astolat (stem: **asto–**)	*to speak*
davralat (stem: **davra–**)	*to be useful to someone*
drivolat (stem: **drivo–**)	*to die*
ezolat (stem: **ezo–**)	*to learn*
fatilat (stem: **fati–**)	*to insult*
fevelat (stem: **feve–**)	*to thirst, to be thirsty*
garvolat (stem: **garvo–**)	*to hunger, to be hungry*
hakelat (stem: **hake–**)	*to name*

lekhilat (stem: lekhi–)	to taste
marilat (stem: mari–)	to build
nofilat (stem: nofi–)	to wipe
qiyalat (stem: qiya–)	to bleed
rhelalat (stem: rhela–)	to help
sikhtelat (stem: sikhte–)	to spit
thimalat (stem: thima–)	to leak
vindelat (stem: vinde–)	to stab
yanqolat (stem: yanqo–)	to gather
zigerelat (stem: zigere–)	to need

Now you can say a very important phrase:

Anha ezok lekhes Dothraki.
I'm learning Dothraki. (lit.: *I'm learning the Dothraki language.*)

⊕ Culture Note
THE IMPORTANCE OF HORSES

As you have noticed, the Dothraki frequently make reference to riding horses (**hrazef**). Even the deity worshipped by the Dothraki is a horse called the Great Stallion (**Vezhof**). Dothraki fight battles on horseback and ride to get around the grassy plains of Essos known as the Dothraki Sea (**Havazh Dothraki**). When a **khal** can no longer ride his horse, he is no longer the leader of his khalasar. As a result of the importance of horses to Dothraki culture, there are many idiomatic expressions related to horses and riding. You've already seen the word *to ride* (**dothralat**). Now, let's look at some idiomatic expressions using **dothralat**.

Hash yer dothrae chek?
How are you? (lit.: *Do you ride well?*)

Anha dothrak chek.
I'm fine. (lit.: *I ride well.*)

Dothras chek.
Be cool. (lit.: *Ride well.*)

Anha dothrak she vaesoon.
I'm from the city. (lit.: *I ride from the city.*)

Anha dothrak adakhataan.
I'm about to eat. (lit.: *I ride to eating.*)

Anha dothrak adakhatoon.
I just ate. (lit.: *I ride from eating.*)

Note the different forms **dothralat** takes in each expression. These are different conjugations and voices that you will learn throughout this course.

Verbs: –at Verbs in the Present Tense

You just learned how to conjugate regular –lat verbs in the present tense in Dothraki. Now let's look at –at verbs. To conjugate an –at verb in Dothraki, again, form the stem of the verb by dropping the suffix (–at) and then add these endings:

	SINGULAR	PLURAL
First person	–ak	–aki
Second person	–i	–i
Third person	–a	–i

Let's look at a regular Dothraki –at verb: astat (*to say*). In the present tense, astat (stem: ast–) will conjugate as follows:

	SINGULAR	PLURAL
First person	astak	astaki
Second person	asti	asti
Third person	asta	asti

Now let's look at how this works with the pronouns.

Anha astak.
I say.

Yer asti.
You (sg.) say.

Me asta.
He says.

Kisha astaki.
We say.

Yeri asti.
You (pl.) say.

Mori asti.
They say.

Shafka asti.
You (sg./pl. fml.) say.

Here are some other verbs that conjugate similarly to **astat**:

adakhat (stem: **adakh–**)	*to eat*
addrivat (stem: **addriv–**)	*to kill*
azhat (stem: **azh–**)	*to give*

charat (stem: char–)	to hear
chetirat (stem: chet–)	to canter
chomat (stem: chom–)	to respect
dinat (stem: din–)	to pass
donat (stem: don–)	to shout
eshat (stem: esh–)	to get up
emat (stem: em–)	to smile (at), to approve of
fakat (stem: fak–)	to kick
fatat (stem: fat–)	to slap
frakhat (stem: frakh–)	to touch
gerat (stem: ger–)	to lack
ifat (stem: if–)	to walk
imeshat (stem: imesh–)	to be young
karlinat (stem: karlin–)	to gallop
khezhat (stem: khezh–)	to be sad
lanat (stem: lan–)	to run
lojat (stem: loj–)	to hit
menat (stem: men–)	to be empty
nirat (stem: nir–)	to be full
nithat (stem: nith–)	to feel pain
ostat (stem: ost–)	to bite
qafat (stem: qaf–)	to ask

rochat (stem: roch–)	*to scrape*
shilat (stem: shil–)*	*to go*
tihat (stem: tih–)	*to see*
yarat (stem: yar–)	*to flinch*
zalat (stem: zal–)*	*to want, to hope for*

*Note that shilat and zalat look as if they might be –lat verbs with the respective stems shi– and za–, but we can see from the past tense singular form that the stems are shil– and zal–. Don't worry too much about this, though. Going forward we'll indicate the stem for you in places where it's not obvious.

Verbs: Negation

To make the above verbs negative, you'll need different endings for your conjugation, as well as the negative marker **vos** or **vo** (*no, not*) which is placed before the verb. **Vos** is used before verbs that begin with a vowel, while **vo** is used before verbs that begin with a consonant. For –lat verbs, use the following negative endings:

	SINGULAR	PLURAL
First person	remove final vowel, add –ok	remove final vowel, add –oki
Second person	–o	–o
Third person	–o	–o

Let's see how this works with two –lat verbs, **dothralat** (*to ride*) and **indelat** (*to drink*), since their stems end in different vowels:

	SINGULAR	PLURAL
First person	dothrok indok	dothroki indoki
Second person	dothrao indeo	dothrao indeo
Third person	dothrao indeo	dothrao indeo

For –at verbs, use the following negative endings:

	SINGULAR	PLURAL
First person	–ok	–oki
Second person	–i	–i
Third person	–o	–i

	SINGULAR	PLURAL
First person	astok	astoki
Second person	asti	asti
Third person	asto	asti

Anha vo dothrok.
I don't ride.

Yer vos indeo.
You (sg.) don't drink.

Me vos asto.
He doesn't say.

Kisha vos indoki.
We don't drink.

Yeri vo dothrao.
You (pl.) don't ride.

Mori vos asti.
They don't say.

Verbs: Past Tense

Forming the past tense of verbs in Dothraki is very easy, as the verb doesn't need to agree in person. However, verbs will still conjugate according to number. To form the past tense of positive statements, add nothing to verbs with singular subjects, but add –(i)sh to verbs with plural subjects, as shown below.

AFFIRMATIVE PAST TENSE		
	SINGULAR	**PLURAL**
–lat verbs	— dothra inde	–sh dothrash indesh
–at verbs	— ast char	–ish astish charish

Anha/yer/me dothra.
I/you (sg.)/he/she/it rode.

Kisha/yeri/mori indesh.
We/you (pl.)/they drank.

Anha/yer/me ast.
I/you (sg.)/he/she/it said.

Kisha/yeri/mori charish.
We/you (pl.)/they heard.

For negative past tense statements, begin with the affirmative past tense conjugations and modify them as follows:

NEGATIVE PAST TENSE		
	SINGULAR	PLURAL
–lat verbs	change final vowel to o **dothro** **indo**	change final vowel to o **dothrosh** **indosh**
–at verbs	–o **asto** **charo**	change i to o **astosh** **charosh**

Kisha/yeri/mori vo dothrosh.
We/you (pl.)/they didn't ride.

Anha/yer/me vos indo.
I/you (sg.)/he/she/it didn't drink.

Anha/yer/me vo charo.
I/you (sg.)/he/she/it didn't hear.

Kisha/yeri/mori vos astosh.
We/you (pl.)/they didn't say.

Verbs: Future Tense

Just as with past tense, the future tense of Dothraki verbs is easy to form. For the future tense of verbs beginning with a vowel, simply start with the affirmative or negative present tense conjugation (depending on whether the statement in the future is to be affirmative or negative) and add the prefix v– to the verb. For verbs beginning with a consonant, start with the affirmative present tense conjugation of the verb, then add the prefix a– to the verb in affirmative statements, and the prefix o– to the verb in negative statements.

FUTURE TENSE		
	AFFIRMATIVE	**NEGATIVE**
verbs beginning with vowel	add v to present tense affirmative verb **anha vifak** *I will walk*	add v to present tense negative verb **anha vifok** *I will not walk*
verbs beginning with consonant	add a to present tense affirmative verb **anha adothrak** *I will ride*	add o to present tense affirmative verb **anha odothrak** *I will not ride*

Anha adothrak vaesaan.
I will ride to the city.

Me vos odothrae vaesaan.
He won't ride to the city.

Mori vifi vaesaan.
They will walk to the city.

Kisha vo vifoki vaesaan.
We won't walk to the city.

Expressing *To Be*

In English, we use a copular verb (*to be*) to link a noun or pronoun with another noun phrase or adjective (e.g. *She **is** a teacher. We **are** tired.*) There is no explicit verb in Dothraki meaning *to be*. You can express sentences such as these in Dothraki by putting two nominative nouns (or pronouns) side by side.

mahrazh (*man*) + lajak (*warrior*)

Mahrazh lajak.
The man is a warrior.

To express the negative of *to be* in this context, you simply add the word vos—*no/not*—between the two nouns. In this case, the form vos is invariant, meaning it won't change when it's followed by a vowel or a consonant.

Mahrazh vos lajak.
The man is not a warrior.

To express *to be* with adjectives in Dothraki, you can make an adjective into a verb—called a "stative verb"—by adding the ending –(l)at. Then you simply conjugate the stative verb as you would any other Dothraki verb. Here are some examples:

erinat	*to be kind*
dikat	*to be fast*
fishat	*to be cold*
hajat	*to be strong*
naqisat	*to be small*
zheanalat	*to be beautiful*
zhokwalat	*to be big*

Anha zheanak.
I am beautiful.

Me zhokwae.
He is big.

Shafka vos naqiso.
You (fml.) were not small.

Mori ahaji.
They will be strong.

Expressing *To Have*

To express *to have* in Dothraki, you will use the idiomatic expression **mra qora**, which literally means *in hand*.

Used in conjunction with nouns in the nominative case, it means *to have*. The noun appearing before **mra qora** is the object being possessed.

Arakh mra qora.
I have an arakh./He has an arakh./They have an arakh., etc.

This expression literally means *an arakh is in (one's) hand*. The context will determine the possessor.

Imperatives

The imperative mood expresses commands or requests. In Dothraki there are two ways to express the imperative mood. The informal imperative is used for requests while the formal imperative is used for commands.

The informal imperative is expressed in affirmative statements by adding –(a)s (–as to verb stems ending in a consonant and –s to stems ending in a vowel).

Lekhis jin lamekh.
Taste this mare's milk.

In negative requests, remove the final vowel and add –os.

Vo liwos haz hrazef.
Don't tie that horse down.

For formal orders or commands, add –i to verb stems ending in a consonant (–at verbs), and use the bare verb stem if it ends in a vowel (–lat verbs).

Inde!
Drink!

Loji!
Run!

In negative statements, the –i or stem vowel ending will change to an –o.

Vos asto!
Don't speak!

Noun Animacy

In Dothraki, whether a noun is animate or not determines its case ending. In English, we distinguish between animate and inanimate nouns when we use a third person pronoun. So, for instance, in English you say *It's on the sofa* to refer to a book on the sofa, but *She's on the sofa* to refer to a female (animate) person on the sofa.

In Dothraki, the distinction is not as clear cut as it is in English. While living, self-aware individuals like the "she" in the above example are animate, so are some other things that would not be considered animate in English. By the same token, some things that would be considered animate in English are not in Dothraki. You'll get the hang of it once you start seeing these nouns in action, but for now, just memorize the distinction.

ANIMATE NOUN EXAMPLES	ENGLISH
rizh	son
ashefa	river
lajak	warrior
nhare	head

INANIMATE NOUN EXAMPLES	ENGLISH
rhiko	stirrup
zhavvorsa (also zhavorsa or jhavorsa)	dragon
hlofa	wrist, ankle
hrazef	horse

In all vocabulary lists in this course, inanimate nouns will be listed as "i.n." and animate nouns will be listed as "a.n."

Noun animacy will be important when learning how to express possession. It also matters when forming plurals. Only animate nouns have a plural form, adding –i to nouns ending in a consonant and –si to nouns ending in vowels.

rizhi	sons
ashefasi	rivers
lajaki	warriors
nharesi	heads

Inanimate nouns have the same form whether they are singular or plural. Whether or not an inanimate noun is plural will be determined by context.

As a final note, noun phrases are inflected on the head noun, which is the first noun in the compound or phrase. Consequently when the animacy is listed for a noun phrase, only the animacy of the head noun will be listed. For example, **dosh khaleen** is the word for the council of elder women who advise all Dothraki on spiritual and social matters. **Dosh**, which means *council*, is inanimate; **khaleen**, which means *elder woman*, is animate. The term **dosh khaleen**, then, is inanimate as a whole. For example, if you wanted to say *the advice of the dosh khaleen*, you would say **fonnoya doshi khaleen**, where the genitive –i suffix is attached to **dosh**, and not **khaleen**.

An Introduction to Dothraki Cases

A case is a nominal marker which indicates what grammatical role a given noun plays in the sentence. There are five cases in Dothraki: Nominative, Accusative, Genitive, Allative, and Ablative. You don't need to learn the full usage of all cases to speak basic Dothraki, but just so you have an idea of how some of the cases are used, let's look at each of them.

NOMINATIVE

You have already seen the nominative case, the most basic form of the noun. The nominative is the case used most often when a noun is the subject of a sentence. This is also the dictionary form of nouns; when you see nouns in vocabulary lists, they will be in the nominative case.

NOMINATIVE
arakh *sword/swords*
jano *dog/dogs*
rizh *son*
rizhi *sons*

NOMINATIVE
ashefa *river*
ashefasi *rivers*

ACCUSATIVE

The accusative case is used most often when a noun is the direct object of a sentence. In English, this would be the word *him* in the sentence *I see him*. One would never say *I see he*. Just as *he* must become *him* in English, nouns in Dothraki need to change form when they appear as the object of a verb.

To form the accusative of inanimate nouns, use the nominative form of the word for nouns ending in consonants, and remove the final vowel of nouns ending in a vowel.

NOMINATIVE	ACCUSATIVE
arakh *sword/swords*	arakh *sword/swords* (object)
jano *dog/dogs*	jan *dog/dogs* (object)

Some inanimate nouns take –e in the accusative. These include nouns whose stems end in g, w, or q, as well as nouns that end in certain consonant clusters. Since this group of inanimate nouns isn't entirely predictable, they will be labeled as "Class B" nouns in the lexicon.

For animate nouns, add –es to the noun stem for singular nouns, and, for plural nouns, add –is to consonant-ending nouns and –es to vowel-ending nouns.

NOMINATIVE	ACCUSATIVE
rizh *son*	rizhes *son* (object)
rizhi *sons*	rizhis *sons* (object)
ashefa *river*	ashefaes *river* (object)
ashefasi *rivers*	ashefaes *rivers* (object)

GENITIVE

The genitive case is used most often when expressing possession, as in *the khal's sword*. For inanimate nouns, the genitive case is formed by adding –**i** to the noun stem.

NOMINATIVE	GENITIVE
arakh *sword/swords*	arakhi *sword's/swords'*
jano *dog/dogs*	jani *dog's/dogs'*

For animate nouns, the genitive is formed by adding –(s)i to the end of the noun, regardless of whether the noun is singular or plural.

NOMINATIVE	GENITIVE
rizh *son*	rizhi *son's*
rizhi *sons*	rizhi *sons'*
ashefa *river*	ashefasi *river's*
ashefasi *rivers*	ashefasi *rivers'*

ABLATIVE

The ablative case is a locative case, meaning it indicates location. The ablative case generally indicates motion away from the noun. It is also used in expressing inalienable possession. A noun is possessed inalienably when it can't (or ordinarily wouldn't) be removed from its possessor. Examples of inalienably possessed nouns are the body parts of an animal, the branches of a tree, the roof of a house, or the hilt of a sword. For more detailed information on possession, please see the section on Expressing Possession.

To form the ablative case of an inanimate noun, add –**oon** to the noun stem.

NOMINATIVE	ABLATIVE
arakh *sword/swords*	arakhoon *from the sword/from the swords*
jano *dog/dogs*	janoon *from the dog/from the dogs*

To form the ablative case of an animate noun, add –(s)oon to singular nouns, and –(s)oa to plural nouns.

NOMINATIVE	ABLATIVE
rizh *son*	rizhoon *from the son*
rizhi *sons*	rizhoa *from the sons*
ashefa *river*	ashefasoon *from the river*
ashefasi *rivers*	ashefasoa *from the rivers*

ALLATIVE

The allative case is another locative case; it indicates motion towards a noun. For many verbs, it also indicates an indirect object, recipient, or goal.

To form the allative case of an inanimate noun, add –aan to the noun stem.

NOMINATIVE	ALLATIVE
arakh *sword/swords*	arakhaan *to the sword/to the swords*
jano *dog/dogs*	janaan *to the dog/to the dogs*

To form the allative case of an animate noun, add –(s)aan to singular nouns, and –(s)ea to plural nouns.

NOMINATIVE	ALLATIVE
rizh *son*	**rizhaan** *to the son*
rizhi *sons*	**rizhea** *to the sons*
ashefa *river*	**ashefasaan** *to the river*
ashefasi *rivers*	**ashefasea** *to the rivers*

Certain prepositions will also dictate which case a noun will take, but you will learn these usages in more advanced Dothraki studies.

PRONOUNS

Pronouns in Dothraki also take cases, since they stand in for nouns. Let's take a look at the personal pronouns in all five Dothraki cases.

	I
Nominative	anha
Accusative	anna
Genitive	anni
Ablative	anhoon
Allative	anhaan

	YOU (SG.)
Nominative	yer
Accusative	yera
Genitive	yeri
Ablative	yeroon
Allative	yeraan

	YOU (FORMAL)
Nominative	shafka
Accusative	shafka
Genitive	shafki
Ablative	shafkoa
Allative	shafkea

	HE/SHE/IT
Nominative	me
Accusative	mae
Genitive	mae
Ablative	moon
Allative	maan

	WE
Nominative	kisha
Accusative	kisha
Genitive	kishi
Ablative	kishoon
Allative	kishaan

	YOU (PL.)
Nominative	**yeri**
Accusative	**yeri**
Genitive	**yeri**
Ablative	**yeroa**
Allative	**yerea**

	THEY
Nominative	**mori**
Accusative	**mora**
Genitive	**mori**
Ablative	**moroa**
Allative	**morea**

Expressing Possession

You can express possession using either possessive modifiers, or with the genitive or ablative cases of nouns.

Possessive modifiers are words used before nouns to express possession. *My, your, his* in English are examples of possessive modifiers. In Dothraki, these are formed by the genitive case or the ablative case. The genitive case is used for most nouns, but inalienable possession, such as body parts, is formed using the ablative case.

NOMINATIVE	GENITIVE	ABLATIVE
anha *I*	anni *my*	anhoon *my*
yer *you (sg. fam.)*	yeri *your (sg. fam.)*	yeroon *your (sg. fam.)*
shafka *you (formal)*	shafki *your (formal)*	shafkoa *your (formal)*
me *he/she/it*	mae *his/her/its*	moon *his/her/its*
kisha *we*	kishi *our*	kishoon *our*
yeri *you (pl. fam.)*	yeri *your (pl. fam.)*	yeroa *your (pl. fam.)*
mori *they*	mori *their*	moroa *their*

Note that in Dothraki, the possessive modifier follows the noun.

okeo anni
my friend

qora anhoon
my hand/arm

okre yeri
your (sg.) tent

tihi yeroon
your (sg.) eyes

arakh mae
his/her arakh

noreth moon
his/her hair

You can also use the genitive or ablative case of any noun (not just a pronoun) to express possession, using the same rules as above. To form the genitive case for inanimate nouns, add the suffix −i to the stem of the noun. To form the genitive case of animate nouns, add the suffix −(s)i to the end of the word. This will be the same for both plural and singular nouns.

NOMINATIVE	GENITIVE
jano *dog/dogs*	jani *dog's/dogs'*
lajak *warrior*	lajaki *warrior's/warriors'*

To form the ablative case of inanimate nouns, add the suffix –**oon** to the stem of the noun. To form the ablative case of animate nouns, add the suffix –**(s)oon** to singular nouns, and –**(s)oa** to plural nouns.

NOMINATIVE	ABLATIVE
jano *dog/dogs*	janoon *dog's/dogs'*
lajak *warrior*	lajakoon/lajakoa *warrior's/warriors'*

Jahaki lajakoa neaki.
The warriors' braids are long.

Compare that sentence with this one below, in which the possession is no longer inalienable.

Jahaki lajaki vekhi she sorfosor.
The warriors' braids are on the ground. (Because they have been cut off.)

Sometimes possessives are left off entirely if the possessor is obvious based on the context of the sentence and the possessed noun is inalienably possessed.

Anha vaddrivak yera m'asikhtek khadokh.
I will kill you and spit on your body. (lit.: I will kill you and spit on the corpse.)

There is an important new word in the above sentence: **ma** (seen here in its contracted form, **m'**). **Ma** is the Dothraki word for *and*.

Numbers

Let's look at how to count in Dothraki. First, we'll start with 0–10:

som	*0*
at	*1*
akat	*2*
sen	*3*
tor	*4*
mek	*5*
zhinda	*6*

fekh	7
ori	8
qazat	9
thi	10

For the teens, just add the suffix –thi to the base number.

atthi	11
akatthi	12
senthi	13
torthi	14
mekthi	15
zhindatthi	16
fekhthi	17
oritthi	18
qazatthi	19

Numbers 20 and above are a bit more complex. To form them, add the prefix ch– to base numbers beginning with a vowel, or chi– to numbers beginning with a consonant.

chakat	20
chisen	30
chitor	40

chimek	50
chizhinda	60
chifekh	70
chori	80
chiqazat	90

And above 100, add the suffix ken to the base number.

ken	100
akatken	200
senken	300
torken	400
mekken	500
zhindaken	600
fekhken	700
oriken	800
qazatken	900

1,000 is dalen, and 1,000,000 is yor.

Adjectives

Let's look at a few common adjectives.

davra	useful/good
dik	fast
fish	cold
haj	strong
naqis	small
zheana	beautiful
zhokwa	big

Adjectives follow the noun they are describing.

arakh davra
a good arakh

hrazef dik
a fast horse

lajak haj
a strong warrior

You've already seen some of these adjectives earlier in this course in the form of stative verbs—**dikat, fishat, hajat, naqisat, zheanalat, zhokwalat**—which are formed from the adjectives above. We can look now at how adjectives work with nouns, both as qualifying adjectives and as stative verbs.

arakh davra
a good arakh

Arakh davrae.
The arakh is good.

Arakh davra vos oflecha.
A good arakh will not be dull.

hrazef dik
a fast horse

Hrazef dik.
The horse was fast.

Hrazef dik adavrae.
The fast horse will be good.

khaleesi zheana
the beautiful khaleesi

Khaleesi zheanae.
The khaleesi is beautiful.

Khaleesi zheana afisha.
The beautiful khaleesi will be cold.

Adjectives will agree in number with plural animate nouns.

lajak haj, lajaki haji
a strong warrior, strong warriors

Lajaki haji.
The warriors are strong.

Lajaki haji dikish.
The strong warriors were fast.

Note in the following examples that when using both an adjective and a possessive modifier, the adjective will come between the noun and the possessive modifier.

Arakh davra mae has.
His good sword was sharp.

Hrazef davra khali adiki.
The khal's good horses will be fast.

Adjectives also agree in case, where possible. Singular adjectives that end in a consonant take the –a suffix to indicate that they modify a noun in some case other than the nominative. When the noun being modified by the adjective is plural, it takes the plural –i instead of the non-nominative –a, regardless of the case of the noun.

Qorasi khaleesisoon haja fishish.
The strong khaleesi's arms were cold.

Jahaki lajakoa haji neakish.
The strong warriors' braids were long.

Making Comparisons

In English, adjectives can take the suffix *–er* to indicate that its quality is greater than that of another entity, and *–est* to indicate that its quality is superior. In Dothraki, there are four levels of comparison (not including the neutral adjective). These can be applied to both verbs and adjectives.

haj	*strong*
ahajan	*stronger*
ahajanaz	*strongest*
ohajan	*less strong*
ahajanoz	*least strong*

erin	*kind*
aserinan	*kinder*
aserinanaz	*kindest*
oserinan	*less kind*
aserinanoz	*least kind*

Let's look at a few examples of how this works, using the above adjectives and the noun **mahrazh** (*man*).

mahrazh haj/mahrazh erin
strong man/kind man (neutral adjective)

mahrazh ahajan/mahrazh aserinan
stronger man/kinder man (comparative)

Mahrazh ahajana yeroon. Mahrazh aserinana yeroon.
The man is stronger than you. The man is kinder than you.

mahrazh ahajanaz/mahrazh aserinanaz
strongest man/kindest man (superlative)

Mahrazh ahajanaza. Mahrazh aserinanaza.
The man is the strongest. The man is the kindest.

mahrazh ohajan/mahrazh oserinan
less strong man/less kind man (contrastive)

Mahrazh ohajana yeroon. Mahrazh oserinana yeroon.
The man is less strong than you. The man is less kind than you.

mahrazh ahajanoz/mahrazh aserinanoz
least strong man/least kind man (sublative)

Mahrazh ahajanoza. Mahrazh aserinanoza.
The man is the least strong. The man is the least kind.

Using Adverbs

Adverbs are words that describe how, where, or when something is done. There are various types of adverbs: manner, time, place, frequency, and degree. Let's look at some pure adverbs in Dothraki.

akka	*also, too, as well, even, even so*
akkate	*both*
alle	*further, farther*
aranne	*carelessly*
ate	*first*
chek	*well*
chekosshi	*very well, excellently*
disse	*only, simply, exclusively, just*
evoon	*all along, the whole time, from the beginning*
ha nakhaan	*finally, last, ultimately*
hezhah	*far, off, hence*
lekhaan	*enough, sufficiently*
nakhaan	*completely, totally, fully*
niyanqoy	*together*
norethaan	*completely*
qisi	*near, nearby, close; soon*
san	*much, a lot, many*
sanekhi	*a lot, many times*

save	*again*
sekke	*too (much), too much; so, really, very*
sille	*next*
vosan	*not much, not a lot*
yath	*up, upward, upwards, high*
yomme	*across*
zhorre	*own*
zohhe	*down, downward, downwards*
zolle	*a little bit, a bit, a small amount, some*

In Dothraki, adverbs can also be derived from nouns or adjectives. Note the formation using the preposition ki (*by*) and the genitive form of nouns.

athhajar *strength*	k'athhajari *strongly* (lit.: *by strength*)
athjilar *correctness*	k'athjilari *correctly* (lit.: *by correctness*)
athlavakhar *loudness*	k'athlavakhari *loudly* (lit.: *by loudness*)

Adverbs tend to be used at the end of a sentence, but temporal and spatial adverbs can be fronted for emphasis.

Demonstratives

Demonstratives are words used to indicate *this* or *that, these* or *those*. In Dothraki, demonstratives work both as demonstrative adjectives and demonstrative pronouns. Let's first look at the demonstrative adjectives.

DEMONSTRATIVE ADJECTIVES

In Dothraki, demonstratives mark distance from the speaker and listener: *this, that, that over there*. Different from adjectives, demonstrative adjectives come *before* a noun: *this man, that horse*.

jin *this/these* (near the speaker)	haz *that/those* (close to the listener)	rek *that/those over there* (far from both speaker and listener)
jin ifak/ifaki *this foreigner/these foreigners*	haz ifak/ifaki *that foreigner/those foreigners*	rek ifak/ifaki *that foreigner over there/those foreigners over there*
jin hrazef *this horse/these horses*	haz hrazef *that horse/those horses*	rek hrazef *that horse over there/those horses over there*

Jin lamekh davrae.
This mare's milk is good.

Haz hrazef dika.
That horse is fast.

Rek ifaki vo haji.
Those foreigners are not strong.

Locational adverbs meaning *here*, *there*, and *over there* can be derived from these demonstrative adjectives by doubling the final consonant of the root and adding –e.

jinne *here* (near the speaker)	hazze *there* (close to the listener)	rekke *over there* (far from both speaker and listener)
Ifak kovara jinne. *A foreigner stands here.*	**Ifak kovara hazze.** *A foreigner stands there.*	**Ifak kovara rekke.** *A foreigner stands over there.*

DEMONSTRATIVE PRONOUNS

Demonstrative pronouns, unlike demonstrative adjectives, are modified based on animacy and plurality. Let's first look at the animate demonstrative pronouns in the nominative case.

ANIMATE		
jinak *this* (near the speaker)	**hazak** *that* (close to the listener)	**rekak** *that over there* (far from both speaker and listener)
jinaki *these* (near the speaker)	**hazaki** *those* (close to the listener)	**rekaki** *those over there* (far from both speaker and listener)

Now let's look at the inanimate demonstrative pronouns in the nominative case. Note that the inanimate demonstrative pronouns stay the same regardless of whether they are referring to a singular object or plural objects.

INANIMATE		
jini *this/these* (near the speaker)	**hazi** *that/those* (close to the listener)	**reki** *that/those over there* (far from both speaker and listener)

Let's now look at the demonstrative pronouns in all cases.

THIS/THESE			
	SINGULAR ANIMATE	PLURAL ANIMATE	INANIMATE
Nominative	jinak	jinaki	jini
Accusative	jinakes	jinakis	jin
Genitive	jinaki	jinaki	jini
Ablative	jinakoon	jinakoa	jinoon
Allative	jinakaan	jinakea	jinaan

THAT/THOSE			
	SINGULAR ANIMATE	PLURAL ANIMATE	INANIMATE
Nominative	hazak	hazaki	hazi
Accusative	hazakes	hazakis	haz
Genitive	hazaki	hazaki	hazi
Ablative	hazakoon	hazakoa	hazoon
Allative	hazakaan	hazakea	hazaan

THAT OVER THERE/THOSE OVER THERE			
	SINGULAR ANIMATE	PLURAL ANIMATE	INANIMATE
Nominative	rekak	rekaki	reki
Accusative	rekakes	rekakis	rek
Genitive	rekaki	rekaki	reki
Ablative	rekakoon	rekakoa	rekoon
Allative	rekakaan	rekakea	rekaan

Arakh jinaki hasa.
This one's arakh is sharp.

Jahak hazakoon neaka.
That one's braid is long.

Vovi rekaki meshish.
The weapons belonging to those (people) over there were new.

LESSON 4

VOCABULARY

4: Vocabulary

People

khal (a.n.)	*the leader of a Dothraki horde,* *king* (Please note that there are multiple pronunciation variants; you will hear both khal and kal.)
khaleesi (a.n.)	*queen, wife of a* khal (Please note that there are multiple pronunciation variants; you will hear khal-eh-si, khal-ee-si and ka-lee-si.)
khalakka (a.n.)	*prince, son of a* khal
khalakki (a.n.)	*princess, daughter of a* khal
khalasar (a.n.)	*a horde loyal to a single* khal
khasar (a.n.)	*small group of protectors,* *bloodriders, generals*
khas (a.n.)	*short for* khasar
khasar khaleesi (a.n.)	*queen's guard,* khaleesi's guard
ko (a.n.)	*bodyguard*
dozgosor (a.n.)	*enemy horde, one's own* khalasar (slang)
dosh khaleen (i.n.)	*council of crones; group of* *widowed* khaleesisi

dothrakhqoyi (i.n.)	*bloodrider*
khaleessiya (i.n.)	*hand maiden*
qoy qoyi (i.n.)	*blood of my blood*
lajak (a.n.)	*fighter, warrior*
vezhak (a.n.)	*horse lord*
lajasar (a.n.)	*army*
kemik (a.n.)	*ally*
okeo (a.n.)	*friend*
dozgo (i.n., class B)	*enemy*
jaqqa rhan (i.n., class B)	*mercy men, those who put the dying out of their misery*
awazak (a.n.)	*screamer*
ifak (a.n.)	*foreigner*
fonakasar (a.n.)	*hunting party*
idrik (a.n.)	*leader of a* **fonakasar**, *a hunting party*
koalak (a.n.)	*healer*
maegi (i.n., class B)	*witch, sorceress*
vafik (a.n.)	*lamb girl*
zafra (i.n., class B)	*slave*
azzafrok (a.n.)	*slaver*
jerak (a.n.)	*trader, merchant*
jerak sewafikhaan (a.n.)	*wine merchant*

You probably also want some vocabulary for talking about your various family members.

rhojosor (a.n.)	*family*
ave (a.n.)	*father*
mai (a.n.)	*mother*
rizh (a.n.)	*son*
ohara (i.n.)	*daughter*
gaezo (a.n.)	*brother*
inavva (a.n.)	*sister*
simon (a.n.)	*uncle*
krista (a.n.)	*aunt*
mahrazh (a.n.)	*husband* (common short form of **mahrazhkem**)
chiori (a.n.)	*wife* (common short form of **chiorikem**)
kemak (a.n.)	*spouse*
yalli (i.n., class B)	*child*
simonof (i.n.)	*grandfather*
kristasof (i.n.)	*grandmother*
drane (a.n.)	*mother who is still breast feeding*
siera (a.n.)	*nephew*
janise (a.n.)	*niece*

leishak (a.n.)	orphan (lit.: *little lost one*)
kim (a.n.)	*ancestor*

War Terms

athvilajerar (i.n.)	*war*
vov (a.n.)	*weapon*
arakh (i.n.)	*curved Dothraki sword*
loqam (i.n.)	*arrow*
kohol (i.n.)	*bow*
orvik (i.n.)	*whip*
ize (i.n.)	*poison*
ziso (i.n.)	*wound*
athdrivar (i.n.)	*death*
khadokh (i.n.)	*corpse*
shor tawakof (a.n.)	*armor (foreigner's knight's armor)* (lit.: *steel dress*)
athohharar (i.n.)	*collapse, defeat*
najahak (a.n.)	*victor, winner*
najah (adj.)	*victorious*
najahheya (i.n.)	*victory in battle*
qorasokh (i.n.)	*prize, spoils*

athrokhar (i.n.)	*fear*
filkak (a.n.)	*coward*
qosarvenikh (i.n.)	*lie, trap, deception*
verven (adj.)	*violent*

And now let's look at some verbs used for fighting.

addrivat	*to kill*
arraggat (class B)	*to choke*
assolat	*to command*
atthasat	*to defeat* (insulting), *to make someone/something fall*
azzafrolat	*to enslave*
azzisat	*to harm someone*
fakat	*to kick; to kick at* (when followed by noun in allative case)
fatat	*to slap; to slap at* (when followed by noun in allative case)
fatilat	*to insult; to throw an insult at* (when followed by noun in allative case)
kaffat (class B)	*to crush*
lajat	*to fight*
lojat	*to hit; to hit at* (when followed by noun in allative case)

najahat	*to be victorious*
ovvethat	*to shoot (with a bow), to throw*
qoralat	*to seize, to hold*
saqoyalat	*to be bloody*
vijazerat	*to protect*
vindelat	*to stab; to stab at* (when followed by noun in allative case)
zisat	*to be hurt*

The Human Body

nhare (a.n.)	*head*
hatif (i.n.)	*face*
noreth (i.n.)	*hair*
chare (i.n.)	*ear*
tih (a.n.)	*eye*
riv (i.n.)	*nose*
gomma (a.n.)	*mouth (of a person)*
lekh (i.n.)	*tongue*
qora (a.n.)	*arm/hand*
torga (i.n., class B)	*stomach*
rhae (a.n.)	*foot/leg*

qoy (i.n.)	*blood*
tolorro (i.n.) (accusative: tolor)	*bone*
kher (i.n.)	*flesh*
meso (i.n.)	*muscle*
ilek (i.n.)	*skin*
zhor (a.n.)	*heart*

Here are some words related to the body's aches and pains.

annithat	*to hurt*
athnithar (i.n.)	*pain*
athmharar (i.n.)	*ache, soreness*
mhari (i.n.)	*headache*
ziso (i.n.)	*wound*
qiya (adj.)	*bleeding*
Anha nithak.	*I'm in pain.*
Rhae annitha anna.	*My foot hurts. (lit.: The foot pains me.)*
Vorto annitha anna.	*My tooth hurts.*
Nhare annitha anna.	*My head hurts.*
Mhari vekha m'anhoon.	*I have a headache.*

Horses

Because horses are so important to Dothraki culture, there are many words related to horses.

hrazef (i.n.)	*horse*
nerro (i.n.) (accusative: ner)	*foal*
lame (a.n.)	*mare*
hrazef chafi (i.n.)	*mustang, a horse that used to be tame*
jedda (i.n.) (accusative: jed)	*pony*
sajo (a.n.)	*steed, mount*
vezh (a.n.)	*stallion*
manin (a.n.)	*young male horse*
dothrakh (i.n.)	*ride*
dothrak (a.n.)	*rider*
sajak (a.n.)	*rider* (lit.: *mounted one*)
eve (i.n.)	*tail*
javrath (i.n.)	*reins*
darif (i.n.)	*saddle*
rhiko (i.n.)	*stirrup*
nozho (i.n.)	*chestnut*
cheyao (a.n.)	*dark bay*
ocha (i.n.)	*dun*

qahlan (i.n.)	*palomino*
messhih (i.n.)	*perlino*
chetirat	*to canter; to canter beside* (when followed by noun in the genitive)
gorat	*to charge a horse*
javrathat	*to rein, to check or guide a horse with the reins*
dothralat	*to ride; to ride beside* (when followed by noun in the genitive)
drogat (class B)	*to drive (an animal)*
hezhahat	*to travel*
vidrogerat	*to ride*
karlinat	*to gallop; to gallop beside* (when followed by noun in the genitive)
sajat	*to mount*
Soroh!	*Halt!* (when talking to a horse)
Hosh!	*Giddyup!*
Affa!	*Woah!*

Food

Let's look at some words for food in Dothraki.

hadaen (i.n.)	*food*
gavat (i.n.)	*meat*
zhifikh (i.n.)	*dry, salted meat*
alegra (i.n., class B)	*duck*
vafi (i.n.)	*lamb*
qifo (i.n.)	*pork*
nindi (i.n.)	*sausage*
ninthqoyi (i.n.)	*blood sausage*
zhif (i.n.)	*salt*
gizikh (i.n.)	*honey*
mesina (i.n., class B)	*soup*
lashfak (i.n.)	*stew*
vitteya (i.n.)	*feast*

Of course, with your meal, you may also want something to drink.

lamekh ohazho (i.n.)	*mare's milk* (fermented or plain)
lamekh (i.n.)	*mare's milk* (fermented or plain)(short form)
eveth (i.n.)	*water*

If you want to talk about eating, you'll need some food related verbs:

adakhat	*to eat*
indelat	*to drink*
tat lanlekh	*to continue to eat something because of the taste*
jolinat	*to cook*
vadakherat	*to feed*
garvolat	*to grow hungry; to hunger for* (when followed by a noun in the ablative)
lekhilat	*to taste*
fevelat	*to thirst; to thirst for* (when followed by a noun in the ablative)
nakhaan	*to be full* (lit.: *to stopping*)

⊕ Culture Note
FOOD

While the Dothraki horses may live off the grass of the plains in the Dothraki Sea, the Dothraki do not eat grass. Instead, they rely on a steady diet of horse meat—**gavat** or **zhifikh** if it is the dried salted version—and fermented mare's milk, **lamekh**. Dothraki do not shy from eating raw meat, though they will not touch rotten food. Pregnant women are encouraged to eat a raw horse's heart, ripped straight from the animal; Dothraki believe that this will help the fetus. Blood sausages (**ninthqoyi**) and blood pie (**fosokhqoyi**) are also staples of Dothraki cuisine.

Hunting

fonak (a.n.)	*hunter*
fonakasar (a.n.)	*hunting party*
idrik (a.n.)	*leader of the hunt*
fonat	*to hunt*
drogat (class B)	*to drive (animals)*
vadakherat	*to feed*
ovethat	*to fly*
govat	*to mate (animals), to breed*
zorat	*to roar*
ogat (class B)	*to slaughter*
ivezho (i.n., class B)	*beast*
ivezh (adj.)	*wild*
kadikh (i.n.)	*captured animal, not yet tamed*
shim (adj.)	*tame*
drogikh (i.n.)	*herd*
haesh (i.n.)	*spawn*
oggo (a.n.)	*head (of an animal)*

hoska (i.n.)	*mouth (of an animal)*
memzir (i.n.)	*bird noise, "tweet"*
felde (i.n.)	*wing*
feldekh (i.n.)	*feather*
eve (i.n.)	*tail*
chiva (i.n.)	*horn*
jahak (a.n.)	*lion's mane*
hem (i.n.)	*fur*
hemikh (i.n.)	*pelt*
kher (i.n.)	*skin (of an animal)*
kherikh (i.n.)	*leather*
dozgikh (i.n.)	*animal carcass*

Nature

sorfosor (a.n.)	*earth*
vorsa (a.n.)	*fire*
eveth (i.n.)	*water*
shekh (i.n.)	*sun*
jalan (a.n.)	*moon*
shierak (a.n.)	*star*
shekhikh (i.n.)	*light*

ramasar (a.n.)	*land, country, plain(s)*
havazh (i.n.)	*sea*
ashefa (a.n.)	*river*
krazaaj (i.n.)	*mountain*
hranna (i.n.) (accusative: hran)	*grass*
feshith (a.n.)	*tree*
sondra (i.n., class B)	*obsidian (dragon glass)*

Question Words

kifinosi	*how*
affin	*when*
finne	*where*
fin	*who* (pron.)
fini	*what* (pron.)
kifindirgi	*why*

Useful Verbs

adakhat	*to eat*
astolat	*to talk, to speak*
charat	*to hear*

charolat	*to listen*
davralat	*to be useful*
dirgat (class B)	*to think*
elat (stem: e–)	*to go*
essalat	*to return*
ezolat	*to learn*
ezzolat	*to teach*
hajolat	*to grow strong*
indelat	*to drink*
jadat	*to come*
jadolat	*to arrive*
nakhat	*to stop*
nesat	*to know (information)*
nesolat	*to learn (information)*
rivvat (class B)	*to smell*
shilat (stem: shil–)	*to know (a person)*
thirat	*to live*
tihat	*to see, to look*
vimithrerat	*to camp, to rest*
vineserat	*to remember*
yolat (stem: yol–)	*to be born*
zalat (stem: zal–)	*to hope for, to want*

zhikhat	to be sick
zhilat (stem: zhil–)	to love
zigerelat	to need, to require

Useful Adjectives

has	sharp
flech	dull
neak	long
fitte	short
ershe	old
imesh	young
ovah	fat
reddi	skinny (perjorative)
redda	thin, sleek
haj	strong
zhokwa	big
naqis	small
zheana	beautiful (used with animate nouns)
rikh	spoiled, rotten

Colors

virzeth	*red*
veltor	*yellow*
dahaan	*green*
thelis	*blue*
reaven	*purple*
theyaven	*pink*
kazga	*black*
zasqa	*white*
nozhoven	*brown*
shiqeth	*gray*
ao	*dark* (of color [lit.: *deep, as in water*])
dei	*light* (of color [lit.: *shallow, as in water*])

Note that there is no word for *orange*; Dothraki will use either veltor or virzeth to describe the color orange, depending on whether it is closer to yellow or red respectively.

LESSON 5
DIALOGUE

5: Dialogue

Let's listen to a conversation between a Dothraki warrior and a visitor.

Verak:	M'athchomaroon, zhey lajak vezhven!
Lajak:	Athchomar chomakaan, zhey verak.
	Finnoon shafka dothrae meshes?
Verak:	Anha dothrak she khalasaroon Khali Fogo.
Lajak:	Khal Fogo… Jin hake nem nesa k'anni. Me
	ray risse san jahaki. Me nem nesa.
Verak:	Me nem nesa. Khal shafki, zhey Khal Saddo,
	me ray atthas san dozgi. Anha vastok ma
	moon, hash shafka vidrie anna maan.
Lajak:	Kifindirgi anha atak jin ha shafkea?
Verak:	Anha fichak maan m'akat kartakis m'at
	vezhes. Mori ma shari ma haji.
Lajak:	Anha atihak jin hrazef.
Verak:	Anha idrik mora. Shafka laz tihi mora ajjin.
Lajak:	Jini hrazef davra k'athjilari. Jin azho
	achomoe khalaan.
Verak:	Athdavrazar. Kohol davra mra qora ha
	shafkea akka, zhey lajak.
Lajak:	Shafka chomoe anhaan, zhey verak. Anha
	vidrik shafka khalaan kishi.

Verak:	San athchomari shafkea, zhey lajak. Anha adothrak shafki.
Lajak:	Dothralates!

Traveler:	Hello, great Warrior!
Warrior:	Greetings, Traveler. Where are you from?
Traveler:	I'm from the khalasar of Khal Fogo.
Warrior:	Khal Fogo ... That name is known to me. He has cut many braids. It is known.
Traveler:	It is known. Your khal, Khal Saddo, has laid low many enemies. I will speak with him, if you will take me to him.
Warrior:	Why would I do this thing for you?
Traveler:	I bring to him two draft horses and a stallion. They are healthy and strong.
Warrior:	I will see these horses.
Traveler:	I'm leading them. You can see them now.
Warrior:	These truly are fine horses. This gift will honor the khal.
Traveler:	Excellent. I have a bow for you as well, Warrior.
Warrior:	You do me honor, Traveler. I will take you to our khal.
Traveler:	Much respect to you, Warrior. I will ride beside you.
Warrior:	Let's ride!

Take It Further

NEW VOCABULARY

You may have noticed some new vocabulary in the dialogue. Here are some new adverbs you just heard.

san	*many, much*
akka	*as well, too*

You also saw some prepositions.

she	*from*
ki (abbreviated k')	*to*
ma (abbreviated m')	*and, with*
ha	*for*

And a few other words:

hash	*if*
kifindirgi	*why*
ajjin	*now*
laz	*can, be able to*

And note, as well, the use of the formal pronoun shafka.

LESSON 6

EXERCISES

6: Exercises

Here's your chance to practice some of the Dothraki you've learned in this course.

A. Fill in the sentences below with the correct present form of the verb **dothralat**.

1. Anha _____ vaesaan.

   I ride to the city.

2. Me _____ vaesaan.

   He rides to the city.

3. Mori _____ vaesaan.

   They ride to the city.

4. Yer _____ vaesaan.

   You (sg.) ride to the city.

5. Kisha _____ vaesaan.

   We ride to the city.

B. Fill in the sentences below with the correct present form of the verb ifat.

1. Me _____ vaesaan.

   She walks to the city.

2. Kisha _____ vaesaan.

   We walk to the city.

3. Yeri _____ vaesaan.

   You (pl.) walk to the city.

4. Mori _____ vaesaan.

   They walk to the city.

5. Anha _____ vaesaan.

   I walk to the city.

C. Rewrite the sentences from sections A and B to make them negative.

1. _____

   _____

2. _____

   _____

3. _____

_____

4. _____

_____

5. _____

_____

D. Translate the phrases below into Dothraki.

1. *the warrior's arakh* _____

_____

2. *the khal's long braid* _____

_____

3. *my weapon* _____

_____

4. *the water of the river* _____

_____

5. *the screamers' heads* _____

_____

E. Now, translate the following sentences from English into Dothraki.

1. *She is beautiful.*

   _____

   _____

2. *The good horse was fast.*

   _____

   _____

3. *My son is strong.*

   _____

   _____

4. *That man (close to the listener) is a warrior.*

   _____

   _____

5. *The warriors' swords will be sharp.*

   _____

   _____

F. Rewrite the sentences from section E to make them negative.

1. _____

   _____

2. _____

   _____

3. _____

   _____

4. _____

   _____

5. _____

   _____

G. Fill in the correct past-tense form of the indicated verb.

1. **Kisha** _____. (**zhilaṭ**)

   We loved.

2. **Mori** _____. (**vimithrerat**)

   They camped.

3. Me _____. (jasat)

   He laughed.

4. Anha _____. (indelat)

   I drank.

5. Yer _____. (hajolat)

   You (sg.) grew strong.

H. Rewrite the sentences from section G in the future tense and give their corresponding negative future tense forms.

1. _____

   _____

2. _____

   _____

3. _____

   _____

4. _____

   _____

5. _____

_____

ANSWER KEY

A. 1. dothrak 2. dothrae 3. dothrae 4. dothrae 5. dothraki

B. 1. ifa 2. ifaki 3. ifi 4. ifi 5. ifak

C. A: 1. Anha vos dothrok vaesaan. 2. Me vos dothrao vaesaan. 3. Mori vos dothrao vaesaan. 4. Yer vos dothrao vaesaan. 5. Kisha vos dothroki vaesaan. B: 1. Me vos ifo vaesaan. 2. Kisha vos ifoki vaesaan. 3. Yeri vos ifi vaesaan. 4. Mori vos ifi vaesaan. 5. Anha vos ifok vaesaan.

D. 1. arakh lajaki 2. jahak neaka khaloon 3. vov anni 4. eveth ashefasoon 5. nharesi awazakoa

E. 1. Me zheanae. 2. Hrazef davra dik. 3. Rizh anni haja. 4. Haz mahrazh lajak. 5. Vovi lajaki ahasi.

F. 1. Me vo zheanao. 2. Hrazef davra vo diko. 3. Rizh anni vo hajo. 4. Haz mahrazh vos lajak. 5. Vovi lajakoa vos ahasi.

G. 1. verish 2. vimithrerish 3. jas 4. inde 5. hajo

H. 1. Kisha azhilaki. Kisha vos ozhilaki. 2. Mori avimithreraki. Mori vos ovimithreraki. 3. Me ajasi. Me vos ojasi. 4. Anha vindek. Anha vo vindok. 5. Yer ahajoe. Yer vos ohajoe.

Acknowledgements

The Dothraki may not say thank you, but I'm about the furthest thing from a Dothraki as a guy can get, so I hope you'll indulge me.

The Dothraki language would not exist without, in inverse order of appearance: the Language Creation Society; David Benioff, D. B. Weiss, and everyone at HBO; and George R.R. Martin. It is on account of their charity that I've been able to help flesh out this corner of the universe George R.R. Martin created.

While I worked on the book—and on translation and everything else—my wife, Erin, was there offering me constant support and proofreading. With a master's in linguistics, she's the only person I trust to catch my mistakes and guide me when I need help. I also want to thank my cat, Keli, for sitting with me patiently while I worked and telling me when to go to bed.

This book itself would not exist were it not for my agent, Joanna Volpe, and my amazing editor, Suzanne McQuade. Though I've long wanted to do a book like this on Dothraki, it was Suzanne who approached me with the idea, and then helped take it from the idea stage to a finished product. She went well above and beyond all of my expectations, and made this book a reality—and for that, I have coined a new Dothraki stem in her honor: **zan,** which means *stable* and *steadfast*. I'd also like to thank the rest of the Living Language team for their enthusiastic support every step of the way.

Special thanks as well to HBO team members Joshua Goodstadt, Janis Fein, Jeff Peters, Cara Grabowski, and Stacey Abiraj.

Finally, I want to thank anyone who over the years has appreciated the fact that a show like *Game of Thrones* went to the trouble to include authentically created languages. A big thank you especially to the original Dothraki fans; this book exists because of your interest and enthusiasm, and is dedicated to you.

About the Author

David J. Peterson was born in Long Beach, California in 1981. He attended UC Berkeley from 1999 to 2003, and received a B.A. in English and a B.A. in Linguistics. He then attended UC San Diego from 2003 to 2006, where he received an M.A. in Linguistics. He's been creating languages since 2000, and working on *Game of Thrones* since 2009. In 2011, he became the alien language and culture consultant for the Syfy original series *Defiance*. In 2013, he joined the crew of the CW's *Star-Crossed* and also Syfy's *Dominion* as a language creator. In 2007, he helped to found the Language Creation Society, of which David has remained a proud member. Recently, he worked with author Nina Post on the Væyne Zaanics language, which features prominently in *The Zaanics Deceit*, the first novel in her Cate Lyr series. He is also the author of *The Art of Language Invention*, to be published by Viking Penguin in 2015.